On the Line

Written by **Kari-Lynn Winters**   Illustrated by **Scot Ritchie**

pajamapress

First published in Canada and the United States in 2021

Text copyright © 2021 Kari-Lynn Winters

Illustration copyright © 2021 Scot Ritchie

This edition copyright © 2021 Pajama Press Inc.

This is a first edition.

10 9 8 7 6 5 4 3 2 1

www.pajamapress.ca   info@pajamapress.ca

The publisher gratefully acknowledges the support of the Canada Council for the Arts and the Ontario Arts Council for its publishing program. We acknowledge the financial support of the Government of Canada through the Canada Book Fund (CBF) for our publishing activities.

Library and Archives Canada Cataloguing in Publication
Title: On the line / written by Kari-Lynn Winters ; illustrated by Scot Ritchie.
Names: Winters, Kari-Lynn, 1969- author. | Ritchie, Scot, illustrator.
Identifiers: Canadiana 20210155191 | ISBN 9781772782189 (hardcover)
Classification: LCC PS8645.I5745 O53 2021 | DDC jC813/.6—dc23

Publisher Cataloging-in-Publication Data (U.S.)
Names: Winters, Kari-Lynn, 1969- author. | Ritchie, Scot, illustrator.
Title: On the Line / written by Kari-Lynn Winters ; illustrated by Scot Ritchie.
Description: Toronto, Ontario Canada : Pajama Press, 2021. | Summary: "Overshadowed by a family of hockey heroes, Jackson Moore is anxious about the high expectations placed on him, and about his own lack of skill. Encouraged by his grandpa to use his own strengths, Jackson becomes a team hero in a new way: by sourcing the equipment they need to enter an important tournament. The book concludes with an author's note about team stewardship, sportsmanship, and community"— Provided by publisher.
Identifiers: ISBN 978-1-77278-218-9 (hardcover)
Subjects: LCSH: Hockey – Juvenile fiction. | Ability -- Juvenile fiction. | Grandfathers – Juvenile fiction. | Teamwork (Sports) – Juvenile fiction. | BISAC: JUVENILE FICTION / Sports & Recreation / Hockey. | JUVENILE FICTION / Social Themes / Self-Esteem & Self-Reliance.
Classification: LCC PZ7.W556On |DDC [E] – dc23

The illustrations were first drawn in pencil, followed by fine line in ink. This was scanned into the computer and finished digitally.

Cover and book design—Lorena González Guillén

Manufactured in China by WKT Company

Pajama Press Inc.
469 Richmond St. E, Toronto, ON M5A 1R1

Distributed in Canada by UTP Distribution
5201 Dufferin Street Toronto, Ontario Canada, M3H 5T8

Distributed in the U.S. by Ingram Publisher Services
1 Ingram Blvd. La Vergne, TN 37086, USA

To the Lynhurst gang, especially
the Moore and Nicholson families
for creating the neighborhood rink
and for inspiring my love of hockey.
And to Chris, Santiago, and Marisol,
who inspire my love of writing about hockey

—K-L.W.

To Nikos Stavroulakis,
a mentor and dear friend
—S.R.

Jackson Moore came from a long line of hockey heroes.

Grandpa, an all-star in his own right, was certain his grandson could follow in his footsteps. He taught the boy how to make a game plan, hold a stick, and pass a puck.

Grandpa reminded him. "You've got Moore in your blood. You'll be great!"

But...

Jackson wasn't so sure.

Grandpa took Jackson to buy skates
and introduced him to Coach Wilson.
The coach smiled at the boy. "Never met
a Moore who wasn't a team hero!"
But...

Jackson wasn't so sure.

At the rink, the team smiled up at Jackson.

"He's a giant," whispered Sonam.

"He's even **MOORE** than I expected," joked Amir.

"He'll be an all-star player!" called Nelson.

But...

Jackson wasn't so sure.

As Jackson stepped onto the ice, he saw hope
in his grandfather's eyes.

He felt amazing, incredible, unstoppable...
then...

Wahhhhh!

Rolling over and over on the ice,
Jackson was a potato on skates.

Coach gathered the team. "Good news—we still have time to practice. Bad news—your participation in the Winterfest Tournament is on the line. We can't play unless everyone has the proper equipment."

Jackson looked around
at his team's mismatched gear.

At dinner, Jackson listened to his family talk about their hockey goals and assists. Their confidence made him feel queasy.

Then Grandpa said something puzzling.
"Jackson, you're good at making game plans."

Jackson thought about that.

He got down to work.

Things were coming together...

...but the practice before the big game did not go well.

"You're sure he's a Moore?" called Amir.

Jackson opened his mouth
to yell back, but nothing came out.
He stormed off the ice.

"You ok?" Grandpa asked. "Probably won't get to play anyway," Jackson grumbled. The two Moores were silent, thinking.

Then Jackson sat up. "I've got it!
I'll make a new game plan."
"That-a-boy!" said Grandpa,
shifting gears.

On game day when the team arrived, Coach Wilson announced, "I have bad news. Some of us couldn't afford the gear. I'm afraid that the game..."

"WILL GO ON!" Jackson blurted, stepping forward. He led everybody to Grandpa's truck.

At game time, the team cheered
as Jackson stepped onto the ice.
Coach Wilson called to Jackson's family,
"Never met a Moore who wasn't a team hero!"

Jackson wobbled a little,
but he gave Grandpa a big thumbs-up.

TEAM STEWARDSHIP

As a child who grew up in the small Southwestern-Ontario city of St. Thomas (just blocks away from the NHL superstar Joe Thornton), I played hockey with my neighbors on an outdoor rink built by my dad and my neighbor's dad (Yes, "Jumbo Joe" did play on that rink with us). There I learned the importance of teamwork and that assists were just as awesome as goals. But what I didn't realize then was that I was also learning about team stewardship: taking care of my friends and neighbors both on and off the ice.

Like Jackson, I wasn't the best skater. I rarely scored goals and I got even fewer assists. But I was a great caretaker for my community. I gathered the teams, brought water for everyone to drink, and swept fallen snow off the ice. I included everyone, even those who weren't so great at playing hockey. I thought about all the players' well-being and helped create a safe space on the ice. Some would say I was a cheerleader for all of the neighborhood kids.

As an adult I learned that being a team steward is more than simply being a team player during a practice or game. It means listening to others, including them, thinking about their safety and needs, remembering their names, understanding what is important to them, and helping them whenever possible. These small steps make a big difference. They strengthen team play.

Even though Jackson is not a good skater, he becomes a true leader. He uses innovative thinking and problem-solving to serve his team. I hope this story inspires other young people to let their stewardship skills shine.

—Kari-Lynn Winters